SPIDER

Janelle Schiecke

Emerald Link Press

CONTENTS

Normal is an illusion. What is normal for
the spider is chaos for the fly.

Charles Addams

For my brother, Bryan

PROLOGUE

The hard illumination from the recessed lighting fixtures in the ceiling created a claustrophobic effect. Shadows cut along the walls at sharp angles, smothering the gray of the stone surfaces. These same shadows played tricks on the facial structures of the two scientists peering down at him.

Their cheekbones shone stark white across their profiles, jutting out from concave eye sockets and sullen cheeks. But when the light hit their eyes, that crazed gleam was unmistakable. The looks of madmen on the precipice of a discovery so utterly malevolent and unthinkable.

They mumbled something to each other, but it was impossible to hear over the chaotic lilts of melodious folk music reverberating in the frigid room. Sparkling notes danced in his head, mocking his futile predicament. Cringing, he balled his hands into fists as he tried to free himself—but it was no use. Several thick, leather straps were cinched around his body, beginning just below his shoulders and continuing down to his calves. What's worse, his head was set into a steel vice. But he could still wiggle it, just a bit. As he did so now, one of the scientists pointed at him.

"Now, David, ve can't have you *move* like zat. You know ve need *complete* compliance."

David whimpered from the operating bed. "I won't... I'll stay steady, I promise! I won't move."

In silent agreement, the other scientist nodded, walking closer to him and reaching a hand down to his head. David's eyes rolled like marbles in his ocular cavities—*oh god*—then he fixed his gaze on the man's face and saw that mischievous grin. There was a loud click, and as the scientist hummed a pleasant tune, the sliding jaw of the vice compressed tighter against David's head.

"NO!" David screamed. "Enough! You're gonna *kill* me!"

The scientist who was still standing at David's side crossed his hands calmly in front of himself, then closed his eyes and nodded. In response, there was another loud click, and the vice clamped its steel jaw down even tighter. Intense pain flared from David's temples to his forehead, a tight band of unrelenting pressure. He cringed in agony and felt the warm tears trickle down his cheeks. They were his only solace, a gentle release of liquid emotion caressing his tender skin.

His chest rose and fell with exertion as his breathing became more labored, and his heart began to palpitate. Then he saw it... that *thing*. They lowered it to his face, and his eyes widened with absolute terror as they prepared it for insertion.

David's harrowing scream came too little too late, for there was nothing that could be done.

THE SPIDER

Jenna swore she'd seen its spindly silhouette when she'd woken up in the middle of the night, standing just inches from her face. It looked like an alien, watching her as she slept. Watching, and waiting... waiting for what? It had to have been a dream, because she hadn't screamed and flung off the bedsheets in hysteria.

But if it wasn't a dream, what then? How long had the spider been sitting there, and where had it gone?

Her skin began to crawl thinking about all of the possible places it could have skittered off to, and fresh goosebumps peppered her skin. She sat up and ruffled her hair, in hopes that if it was wriggling within her tresses, it would fall out.

Arachnophobia was a very real fear for her. She just couldn't shake it. No matter how many times one of her friends told her spiders were more scared of her than she of them, this did nothing to quell her fears. They were so *unnatural*. A head and an abdomen hovering over the ground and scuttling along on eight long and crooked stilts? The stuff of nightmares.

She glanced at her clock on the nightstand, expecting to get up and go about her day, yet the time read 3 a.m. When had she awoken before? Steeling a look at her nearly drawn shades, she observed the darkness beyond. The spider popped into her mind again, and she rushed out of bed, tiptoeing in absolute dread toward the light switch. The thought of stepping on something sinewy and rigid with her bare feet and hearing a slight *pop* made her cringe. With each step, she lowered the ball of her foot very slowly to the floor, so as to avoid a disgusting encounter.

When she made it to the light switch, she flicked it on and threw her back against the wall, seeking any kind of skittering on the wooden oak floor. Wouldn't it blend in, though? Maybe look like scant tumbleweed traversing across the room? Placing her fingers to her lips, she hunched over, considering her options. Did she brave going back to bed with this gross *thing* quite likely still on the loose? Glancing at the Kleenex box on her dresser, she picked it up and began to step forward.

Eyes darting in all directions, she scanned her room for any sign of this alien life-form. Yes, they were aliens as far as she was concerned. She spied nothing on the floor, and nothing on the—

There, on the wall. Straight ahead. There was a dark spot. Jenna began to tremble, wishing now that she'd never even looked for it: blissful ignorance. It was large even from where she stood a few steps away, so the thought of advancing any closer absolutely terrified her. And what if it *jumped*? Did all spiders jump, or just the teeny ones? It was so cruel that they were able to do that. A sick joke by Mother Nature. As if the sight of them wasn't revolting enough.

Bracing herself, she walked very slowly toward the spot on the wall, hoping not to scare it away. As she closed the distance, its eight legs came more into view: those godawful appendages. And this one had a big ol' butt. Resembled that of a Black Widow. *Crunchy.*

Jenna raised the Kleenex box and took a step back with one leg, ready for the death smash. Shaking her head, she mumbled, "Oh, I got ya, you little fucker."

In one fell swoop, she rushed forward, smashing the Kleenex box on the wall and hoping to God she landed it right. Jumping back, she shook her hands and shuffled her feet, staring at the wall. The spider was gone. But the only confirmation was to actually check the bottom of the Kleenex box. Crouching on one leg, with the other she reached her foot out to touch the box. No way she was going too close to it. Maybe she could kick it at just the right angle, flip it bottom-up.

With a swift kick, the box landed against the wall and bounced back, the bottom now facing her. And there, clear as day, was the impression she was looking for: the spider. A greenish liquid had spurted from its abdomen, and its gangly legs were tented inward. *Gross.*

Grabbing her shirt she'd worn yesterday off the top of her dresser, she used the fabric as a buffer between the Kleenex box and her bare hand. Picking it up, she walked over to the garbage can and dropped it in.

The loud thud it made against the plastic surface signaled the end of this charade, and Jenna sighed in relief before jumping back into bed.

Sorry, spider: Wrong place, wrong time.

UNSETTLING SENSATION

Stretching her arms above her head and yawning, Jenna reached over to the nightstand and grabbed her phone. The screen read 10 a.m. Good. She had just enough time to shower before she met up with her friends for lunch at noon. She'd woken up with a slight headache, but it was nothing a Motrin couldn't fix.

Visions of her spider encounter in the early morning hours flashed in her mind, followed by the blind date gone wrong the night before. She'd drunk one too many mixed drinks listening to him drone on about his *lucrative* real estate career. These men were either too nice, too mousy, too assertive, too... Had she set her standards to an unachievable bar?

A tickle swept across her big toe, and Jenna flung the sheets off in a surge of panic. Sweeping her legs into a crisscross position, she wrapped her arms around herself. Her heart had leapt into her chest, and an electric surge of crippling panic coursed through her entire body. This was happening again? How could something so damn small debilitate her to such a crumbling wreck of fraught nerves?

Very carefully, she leaned over and inspected the bedsheets. No moving dark spots, but the corner of the bed was still covered; the corner where her foot had been resting when she'd felt that... tingle.

Leaning over ever so slowly, Jenna reached for the corner of the bedsheets. Her heart began to thump in her chest now. Was there an accomplice, hiding between the sheets, seeking out revenge for its fallen brethren?

Once her fingers found the soft fabric, she flung the covers off and dashed away to her dresser, frantically patting herself down in case it had jumped on her. When she'd ascertained that she was spider free, Jenna tiptoed to her bed. Gazing over the light beige fitted sheet, she found no dark spots.

Not how I wanted to start my day, but here we are.

Relieved, she walked to the bathroom and grabbed a bottle of Motrin. Trudging downstairs, she poured herself a cool glass of water from the fridge dispenser and closed her eyes as the refreshing liquid washed the pills down. Help from this relentless, pounding headache was on its way, and a hot shower was in order next. Jenna tilted her head when she noticed a small flare of pressure in her left ear. It continued for a few seconds, then subsided to a dull ache. Shrugging, she headed upstairs to shower.

The Motrin would take care of everything.

JUST MY LUCK

A cheerful blue sky greeted Jenna as she stepped outside, and she breathed in the invigorating scent of freshly cut grass. If green was a smell, that was it... sharp, earthy, and sweet. The sound of a lawn mower roared in the distance, and she looked to her left to see her neighbor, Mr. Higgins, mowing his lawn. He offered up a friendly wave back as she waved hello, then returned to his routine.

They'd been neighbors since she'd moved into this duplex a year ago, and she couldn't be happier. It was a good setup—a *comfortable* setup. Her landlords, Mr. and Mrs. Miller, lived on the first floor and were lovely as could be. Mrs. Miller was a retired nurse, and Mr. Miller was a retired high school teacher. And since they were in their mid-sixties, this meant Jenna had the luxury of a quiet abode. Well, most of the time...

when the Millers had the occasional spat, it was no holds barred.

What she loved most about where she lived, though, was the quick five-minute walk to town. It was an excuse to get some exercise in and, on days like today, a much-needed pick-me-up. Their downtown had the same charm as most in the Midwest—colorful, quaint, and cozy. And on the agenda for today was a charming Italian bistro that had just opened up.

As she neared the bistro, she spotted her friends Lisa and Marissa sitting outside. They'd all been friends since high school... really the only two people she talked with from high school. Who the hell wants to hold on to those years?

A smile spread across her face when they noticed her and stood up, holding their arms out to embrace her. Lisa and Marissa gave the best hugs, and after the catastrophe that was last night, she needed their good humor too.

"C'mere, you," Marissa cooed. Jenna welcomed her friend's warm embrace, and hugged Lisa in turn. Sitting down, Jenna hung her purse over her chair and looked back at her friends, who were patiently waiting for the news.

"So...? No texts, how'd the date go?" Lisa asked.

Jenna leaned forward and buried her forehead into the backs of her palms. "It went horrible."

"That bad, huh?" Marissa asked.

"Yes, that bad."

"What went wrong?" Lisa asked. "He sounded like a nice enough guy, had his shit together."

"Well... Yes," Jenna replied. "But, I dunno. Just one of those all talk, no listen types. I couldn't even get a word in."

"Maybe he was just trying to impress you?" Lisa asked, cringing and shrugging.

Slapping her palm on the table, Marissa exclaimed, "You don't got time for that. Consider it a one and done and move on."

"One and done? I think I'm just... *done*. Thought I could get back into the game again, but,"—she shrugged—"guess I was wrong."

"It shouldn't have to be a *game*, though," Lisa replied, adjusting her ponytail.

Marissa's eyes grew wide, and she shook her head. Tapping her long, bright red painted nails on the tabletop, she said, "Oh, it's all a game nowadays. All these online dating apps don't help, either. Pretty much just offering up a flavor of the week."

"Two years!" Jenna cried. "Two years we were together." She glanced absentmindedly at her ring finger, to which Marissa took notice.

"Girl, don't be doin' that. First, you don't need a man to feel complete. And second, you *sure* as hell lucked out with Josh."

Jenna's face grew hot, and that stifled rage rose to the surface again. She'd wasted two goddamn years on that piece of shit.

"Listen," Lisa said, leaning over and gently placing her hand on Jenna's. "You told your truth. You aren't ready for marriage, and you're not sure if you want kids. It wouldn't have worked out."

"Yeah, but... I mean, I just feel like a failure. Here I am, early thirties, not even engaged. Not even *dating* anyone."

"Why the rush?" Marissa asked. "You do you. Don't worry about what society dictates." Jenna eyed Marissa's brilliant engagement ring as her friend accentuated her words with a flick of her wrist. That diamond glimmered all the colors of the rainbow when the sun hit it just right. Reminded her of those kaleidoscopes she used to have as a kid. "And don't think I don't see you lookin' at this," Marissa remarked, on cue, as she pointed at her ring.

"I know, I know..." Jenna replied.

Lisa rubbed Jenna's back in gentle circular motions. "Just take a break. Besides, you have that promotion to think about. You really should put all your energy into that."

Jenna shrugged. "Yeah, you're right. No cryin' over spilled milk."

Then she heard it. Wincing, Jenna covered her left ear with her palm.

"What's wrong?" Marissa asked.

"There's... *ringing*," Jenna said, scoffing.

"What? In your *ear*?" Lisa asked.

"Y-yeah," Jenna replied. "And it's pretty loud, what the fuck?"

"Oh, that's just tinnitus. I went through a bout of that a few years ago. It's actually pretty common, lots of people get it."

"Well, then why did I just get it?" Jenna asked, flustered. "Just this very *second*?"

Lisa shrugged. "Dunno. Did you injure it or something?"

"*No*," Jenna replied. "I mean, maybe I slept on it weird? Last night was... well, it was a thing."

"Oh Lordy, what happened now?" Marissa asked, chuckling.

"Well, there was this damn spider. Almost gave me a heart attack, I swear. *You* know how I am with those things."

Marissa cringed in disgust, lifting her hands and wiggling her fingers.

"Ah, they creep in now and then. Can't blame 'em. I'll just throw 'em back outside if they look scary enough." Lisa shrugged.

"Yeah, about that… I don't care. Gave it a good smash with a Kleenex box and went back to bed."

Marissa breathed in sharply, placing a hand over her mouth.

"What?" Jenna asked, sneering.

"That's bad luck, you know. Killin' a spider."

Jenna looked to Lisa, who pursed her lips and nodded in agreement.

"Well," Jenna retorted. "Then bad luck will befall me and hit me hard. 'Cause I never spare those guys. What the…" She covered her ear again, furrowing her brow. The ringing continued.

Lisa noticed Jenna's discomfort. "Listen, sometimes this just starts and there's no rhyme or reason to it. It's messed up, but—I bet it'll go away soon. I've had ringing that lasts just a few seconds, then"—she lifted her hands and pulled them apart, mimicking an explosion—"poof! It goes away."

Jenna pursed her lips and eyed Lisa with a glimmer of contempt. Lisa's soothing demeanor grated harsh against Jenna's nerves. Her friend was acting as if this were normal, but this wasn't normal at all. Lisa caught Jenna's steely gaze.

"Listen," Lisa continued, grabbing her cell that rested on the table. "I'm gonna text you my ENT's info just in case... Oh"—her eyes grew wide as she lifted a finger—"and not for nothin', but mine flared up during allergy season. Which, *hello*, we're in that right now. Gonna be a bad season for pollen this year, too." She winced, shrugging. "Sorry."

Though Jenna heard each word Lisa had said, the ringing persisted, and she knitted her brow as she rubbed the side of her head.

"Don't worry," Marissa replied in kind. "My dad had that on and off for a couple years, and he's fine now. Like Lisa said, it's pretty common."

Again, Jenna listened to Marissa, but the ringing prevented her from responding. She felt so alienated and so utterly alone. As if she were the only one hearing voices, and everyone else was blissfully unaware. Sure, Lisa said she'd had it before but had it been this... LOUD? It resembled the tone of a bell, but drawn out in agonizing monotone.

"The joys of getting older, I guess. Right?" Jenna joked, trying to hide her anxiety with a tilt of her head and a forced smile.

"Ya got that right," Marissa quipped.

"There," Lisa said. "Just texted you his info. He's the best around, you're in safe hands."

Jenna picked up her phone and read Lisa's text, then immediately smirked.

"What?" Lisa asked, flashing her brows.

"His name. Norman *Gates*?"

"Hmm?" Lisa questioned again.

"N-never mind," Jenna said. "Let's just hope he doesn't have any mother issues."

Marissa chuckled and shook her head, nudging Lisa with her elbow. "*Psycho*, Lisa. The book? The movie?"

Lisa slapped her forehead. "Oh, God. Of course. Yeah, um... No, he's definitely not like *that* Norman."

"Well, that's reassuring then." Jenna chuckled as she put her phone back in her purse. The ringing began to decrease in volume, lowering to the sound of a buzzing mosquito. Then it ceased altogether. She took a deep breath in, sitting up straight, and placed a palm to her ear once again. "Guys! It's... it's gone!"

"See?" Marissa beamed. "Nothin' to worry about. Who knows, maybe just some weird flare-up."

"Thank God!" Jenna declared in relief. "Scared the shit outta me. Like I don't have a ton of other stuff to worry about."

"Don't we all," Marissa agreed.

With that, the conversation meandered to movies and TV shows. When the waitress came by to take their orders, they treated themselves to some tasty appetizers and a round of Mojitos. Jenna thought twice about this, having just popped some Motrin this morning. But hell, her liver could handle it.

"At least you're not hearing wind chimes," Lisa said.

"*Wind chimes?* Whaddya mean?"

"You never heard of that urban legend? Ah"—she waved her hand—"never mind. I like the vibe we're at, and the Clatter Man's tale is pretty brutal. I'll save his story for another day."

ZIGGY

It still felt a bit lonely coming home to an empty space—she and Josh had lived together for six months—but Jenna did have her beloved Ziggy. He was a Maine Coon mix she'd adopted a few years ago. All black, with just a little white mark on his chest that resembled a lightning bolt. He hadn't even stirred this morning when she'd put his breakfast out, must have been snoozing real good. He came trotting around the corner as she stepped inside.

"*Hey*, sweetie." Jenna picked him up and nuzzled her cheek against his neck. His purrs were so delicious, rumbling through his entire body. She took comfort in the soothing vibration as she snuggled him close. Though Josh hadn't grown up with animals, he'd taken to this cat pretty quick. Ziggy had quite the personality and even drooled when his purrs hit maximum capacity—turned into an adorable, wet mess.

Still holding Ziggy close, she walked to the couch and plopped down. He stared at her with those moon-shaped, green eyes and kneaded her stomach.

"You like that? You like those chubs?" Jenna quipped. She had a tiny potbelly. Josh had found it cute, while she found it dreadful. "Well, enjoy it while it lasts, because Momma's gonna make sure that goes away *real* soon!"

Jenna massaged Ziggy's soft ears as she looked out the window. The sky had begun to turn, and she spotted some storm clouds rolling in.

Staring back at Ziggy, she smirked and traced the lightning bolt on his chest, then booped his nose. "Did *you* do this?"

Had it called for rain in the forecast? She didn't think so. Lately, it seemed the weather preferred to turn on a dime. That was pretty typical for Ohio, though.

Jenna froze as the ringing in her ear came back... this time a light buzzing, really. Scowling, she bit her lower lip and considered how long she should wait to call the ENT. Would it get worse if she didn't do anything about it? She suspected she could wait it out a little longer. If it indeed was just a seasonal flare-up, it would most certainly die down once allergy season was over. It was barely the end of May, though, and allergy season could last through the summer.

A tinge of worry set in again and she pursed her lips, slumping more into the couch.

Ziggy had snuggled up into an adorable curl on her lap, and she reached for the TV remote. The inclement weather rolling in on this lazy Saturday afternoon called for a good horror movie. Grabbing the blanket draped over the back of the couch behind her, she reclined the seat and covered her legs, then clicked the TV on.

Sound would drown out the persistent ringing. Or at least she hoped it would.

GOALS

Jenna had spent most of her Sunday morning channel surfing, but it was time to dive back into her PowerPoint presentation. Her performance review was tomorrow.

Was the presentation called for? No. Did it convey professionalism and determination? Yes. She'd gone over every topic she would bring up and had rehearsed all possible (well, hopefully all) answers in an exhaustive manner. The PowerPoint slides she'd made had taken several hours to perfect, and Jenna was very proud of what she'd accomplished. Having always harbored a competitive edge, she was going to squash her competition and snag that promotion.

Jenna grabbed a crisp apple from the fruit basket on the kitchen counter and strode to the dining room table. Sitting down, she powered on her laptop and took a bite out of the apple as she waited for her computer to boot up. She'd set her purse on the table last night and, glancing at it now, remembered the doctor contact Lisa had texted her. Closing her eyes, she listened to... silence—beautiful, still, silence. A brief flash of confusion flickered in her mind.

Part of her yearned for an answer as to why she was experiencing tinnitus, but the other (more acceptable) part of her realized this very well was a lost cause. Bodies were weird... random things happened, and sometimes there was really no explanation. And excessive worrying was not something Jenna wanted to entertain right now. If it did come back, maybe she would contact Dr. Gates's office and schedule an appointment. First things first, she needed to make sure this presentation was pristine.

When her laptop's welcome screen appeared, she wiggled her fingers and closed her eyes for a brief moment. When she opened them, Jenna could feel the adrenaline kick in and readied herself to scour this project. She was going to wow everyone and secure that promotion. After all she had been through, she deserved this. Hell, she was *going* to get it—no room for second-guessing.

After logging in, she moved the cursor to Power-Point. Clicking the program open, she navigated to her presentation. The hours she had poured into this showed. Each slide was carefully crafted, easy to comprehend, and comprehensive—no loose ends.

Losing out on this promotion was unacceptable. She was gonna kick ass on Monday.

EYE STRAIN

An aching bladder awoke Jenna from her slumber. Looking at the clock on her nightstand, the time read 2 a.m. She'd recklessly drunk a couple glasses of wine last night—which explained her bladder—and felt hazy. Probably just the alcohol. Fucking Marissa... she had gifted Jenna a bottle for her birthday a few weeks ago and always went for the strong stuff. Should have known.

Flinging the covers off, she opened the door and sauntered to the hallway bathroom. In a stupor, she pulled down her panties and sat on the toilet seat. So fucking *cold*. Wasn't there such a thing as heated toilet seats? How much did they even cost? Leaning over, she rested her elbows on her thighs and relaxed her bladder muscle. Without hesitation, a torrent of pee rocketed to the water below, sounding as if a liquid train had commenced operation. She sighed in relief as her bladder slowly emptied, the immense pressure dissipating.

Still in a haze, Jenna wiped herself dry, pulled her panties up, and walked over to the mirror. She leaned forward, examining the dark circles under her eyes. Aging was such a mockery; you were left watching the grand spectacle of yourself dying slowly day by day. Each new day, you're one step closer to six feet under... or the furnace. To each their own. An extra wrinkle there, a new ache there... the quagmire that is life.

Pulling the skin of her cheeks taut toward her ears, she admired how she looked without that ghastly turkey neck. It really wasn't that bad—*yet*. She never ceased to notice the sagging, paper-thin skin clinging to her mom's neck like flesh-colored plastic wrap. That's where she was headed.

Closing her eyes, Jenna shook her head and ran her fingers through her long, ebony hair. She did have beautiful hair, no doubt about it. So sleek and soft, and that brilliant blue sheen when light hit black tresses just popped. She squinted when the inner corner of her right eye began to itch. Taking off her glasses, Jenna rubbed it vigorously, seeking to quell the itch. Looking in the mirror again, she noticed the redness around her eye. Made sense, she'd just itched it, but... she *felt* something now. There was an accumulation of pressure near her tear duct. Turning to the dimmer switch, she adjusted it to its highest setting, then surveyed her eye again.

She could see something very small near her tear duct, and its pallid color allowed it to nearly blend in with the white of her sclera. After washing her hands, she pulled her lower eyelid down to further examine the pinpoint of blanche.

"What the fuck?" Jenna spoke in a soft whisper.

She'd worn contacts since middle school, so touching her cornea was no biggie. It wasn't *fun* but had ceased to bother her years ago; just routine at this point.

Using her pointer finger, she swiped at the small mass a few times, but it wouldn't budge. In frustration, she threw her arms down at her sides and stared at the ceiling, tapping a foot on the bath mat. This was not what she planned to be doing at two in the morning, but such was her life. Sighing, she assumed the position again and hunched forward, staring into the mirror.

Pulling her lower lid down, she swiped at the small clump again. But this time, it changed shape, and part of it... uncoiled. A very thin, translucent string now hung down near her tear duct, though it was still attached to the small clump wedged in the corner of her eye.

Jenna furrowed her brow and bit her lower lip as she steadily moved her pointer finger to the string. She tapped it very lightly, and as she pulled her finger away, the fiber stuck to her fingertip. Fixating on her reflection in the mirror with a mixture of terror and fascination, she slowly pulled her finger away from her, toward the mirror, and the thread fell from her fingertip.

Looking up at the ceiling again, Jenna winced and shook her hands in a frenzy at her sides as she shifted her weight left and right. Whatever this foreign object was, she had to get it out of her eye.

Once she was ready, she hunched forward again and gripped the string with her pointer finger and thumb. Tugging at it gently led to a feeling of pressure behind her eye, but the mass was uncoiling. Jenna cringed as she gently began pulling at the thread again, witnessing it lengthen in her reflection. The pressure was subtle, but if she pulled with more force, it increased.

Her jaw dropped as the string became longer now—and in the bright light, she noticed it had taken on a crimson sheen. Two inches of the fiber now hung between her fingertips and her eye, and it almost resembled... webbing.

In a panic, Jenna yanked the string hard. There was a *pop* as it detached from within, and the pressure transitioned to a dull throb. Lifting the strand in front of her face to examine it, she noticed something small and red attached to the end of it. Peering at it closer, Jenna realized this was a glistening piece of her own tissue.

And she screamed.

A BRIEF RESPITE

Sitting at her kitchen table, Jenna tapped the sole of her foot on the floor. Resting her elbow on the table-top, she pressed her lips against her fingers. She was staring at her laptop monitor, where she'd pulled up the website for Doctor Gates.

Her eyes darted to the time and date displayed on the upper right-hand corner of the screen, and the time read 7:45 a.m. Their office opened in fifteen minutes, and she was calling that number as soon as it hit 8 a.m.

She'd had some slight ringing this morning, but it had thankfully gone away. Jenna glanced down at the string she'd pulled from her goddamn *eye* last night. In haste, she had grabbed a drinking glass and dropped it within. Picking up the glass, she rotated it to analyze the object more clearly through the smooth, translucent surface.

The piece of tissue at the end of it—*her* tissue—had dried up and resembled a small bit of bloody scrambled egg. The fiber was about three inches in length, with the two inches closest to the tissue a crimson hue. Almost resembled an optic nerve. Kinda like in the movies, when someone's eye is pulled out and the optic nerve comes along with it. Except this was a very threadlike optic nerve, and the eye was miniscule.

Jenna brought the glass closer to her line of sight and noticed some of the fiber had a bluish tinge. Her research last night had concluded that mucus discharge from the eye was either green or yellow. Biting her lower lip, she considered her conundrum.

Based on her near all-nighter spent scouring a bottomless pit of medical websites, she'd come to the conclusion she most likely had an eye infection. An eye infection can lead to mucus in your eye that, when extracted, can resemble string. But then again, mucus discharge from the eye was either green or yellow—not blue.

Also, no research had explained what the tissue at the end of the string might be, or where the tissue was from. To her relief, at least the throbbing had subsided and her eye was no longer itching. But that also meant no eye infection, which brought her back to why this all had happened in the first place.

Maybe she'd just gotten lucky? Some random body discharge, some mindfuckery of the aging process. Whatever the case, her first priority was to contact the ENT and get that appointment scheduled. She had to address this transient ringing. It varied in pitch and was completely random. Sometimes it was as loud as a steady bell, lasting for only a minute or two; sometimes it was incessant clicking that lasted for almost an hour.

She closed her laptop and pushed it away from her, leaning forward and placing her elbows on the table-top. Resting her face in her hands, Jenna closed her eyes... She was completely exhausted. After spending nearly the entire night hunched over in bed, frantically searching for a resolute answer to this experience, her muscles ached and her weary eyes were strained from the harsh glare of blue light in a dim room. Yet, her mind would not settle. When she consciously tried to clear her thoughts, they ran even more rampant—worrying, postulating, suspecting.

Jesus Christ, she needed a goddamn break.

Jenna took a deep breath in and sighed as she leaned back in her chair, arms dangling at her sides. Her presentation was today. She could call in sick, but she *re-*

ally wanted that promotion. She could do this. With enough coffee, she could do anything.

Glancing at the clock display on the microwave, she noticed it was 8:05. *Shit!* Grabbing her laptop, Jenna opened it back up and logged in. She dialed the office number on her cellphone and waited patiently with each passing ringtone.

Squinting her eyes, she bounced the heel of her bare foot nervously against the floor. The third ringtone came and went, and she did *not* want to leave a voice-mail. "C'mon, c'mon, c'mon…"

"Morning, Doctor Gates's office."

The receptionist's chirpy trill ate into every last one of Jenna's shattered nerves. Cringing, she mustered her reply.

"Good morning. I'd like to make an appointment with Doctor Gates, please."

"Wonderful! Are you a current patient or a new patient?"

None of this was wonderful. People went to doctors when they weren't feeling well. Rolling her eyes, Jenna proceeded.

"I'm a new patient."

"Okay, and what's the reason for this visit?"

"I, uh… Well, I've had ear ringing recently, on and off. Sometimes it's really bad, sometimes it's manageable. But none of it's fun."

"Oh dear. Well, let me tell you—Doctor Gates is just wonderful, you'll be in very good hands."

Will I? Isn't that what they're supposed *to say?*

Jenna composed herself before she answered, so as not to sound snide. "Okay, great, thank you. That's good to hear."

She could just hear the receptionist's smile beaming on the other end of the line. Not a care in the world, with no idea how much Jenna's sanity was tearing at the seams. As the receptionist asked for her contact and insurance information, she went through the motions and answered, yearning for this conversation to end. And when it finally came to a close, Jenna smiled in relief.

"Okey dokey," the receptionist chirped on the other end of the line. "I have you down for this Friday at ten a.m. You're really lucky, ya know—there was a last-minute cancellation. Usually new patients have to wait at least a month to see Doctor Gates."

Jenna tightened her lips, eyes wide, then blurted out, "Lucky me!"

"See you then, dear!"

"Sounds good, bye!"

Hanging up, Jenna closed her eyes and smiled again. This Friday... She could make it till this Friday. Five more days. In her grateful reverie, she completely forgot about the time. Glancing at the clock, she noticed it was 8:30.

"Shit!"

Jenna jumped up and headed for the shower. She'd emailed her boss to let him know she would probably be running a little late today, opting for a much smaller sacrifice than calling out sick. At least her presentation was prepared and she could rely on a heavy dose of caffeine to pull her through.

Easy peasy.

CLICK

There had been minimal traffic on the way to work, allowing Jenna to arrive near 9:30. Her presentation was at 10:30, giving her enough time to finish her coffee before meeting with her boss. She powered on her desktop, logged in, and opened her PowerPoint presentation she'd sent to her work email last night. It was too late to make any corrections now, but she still had to give it one more look-through. Biting her lower lip, she clicked through the slides, desperately hoping she didn't miss anything. *Perfect.*

After checking her makeup in her compact mirror, Jenna smiled once more. She had applied it flawlessly, and most importantly it concealed the dark bags under her eyes. Her right eye was still a bit bloodshot near the tear duct, but she'd take what she could get. Looking the part was half the battle. Standing up, she tucked a loose strand of hair behind her ear and pranced in the direction of her boss's office. Her ponytail bounced with each zesty stride. She felt great, she was seeing the doctor soon, she'd nail this meeting, then—

CLICK.

Jenna stopped in her tracks and felt a soft body hit against her from behind.

"Oh, sorry, Jenna," Melanie's sweet and timid voice spoke from behind her.

Jenna turned around and looked at Melanie, smiling and preparing to respond when—

CLICK, CLICK.

"You okay, Jenna?" Melanie asked, head cocked to one side with furrowed brows.

"Y-yes, I'm fine," Jenna lied. "Just thought I forgot something, but it's all good."

The clicks had been so *loud* this time, almost to the tune of a metronome. As she considered this thought, a whirring sound resounded in her ears now. It was muted and resembled the sharp, metallic spin of a dentist drill before it bores into delicate enamel. Thankfully, the dusty smell of shattered enamel and decay didn't follow; nonetheless, it was a paralyzing sensation.

"Okay," Melanie answered. "But if you need anything, lemme know. I *hate* doing performance reviews." She leaned in closer, whispering, "I have Prozac."

"T-thanks, Melanie. I'm really okay, though. Maybe a few last-minute jitters is all."

"Well, the offer still stands," Melanie replied, flashing Jenna a wink. Then she headed toward the break room.

Jenna swallowed down the last bit of confidence she had and pushed ahead. The whir had subsided to a muffled but relentless drone in her ears, but the clicks continued on in the same fashion: unpredictable and jarring. Maybe she should have taken Melanie up on her offer. Stopping in her tracks, Jenna turned around and made way for the break room. She'd take control of the situation; no point in being a martyr.

She was just a few steps away and on the verge of sweet Prozac relief when a large hand clasped down strong on her right shoulder.

"Jenna, you're headed the wrong way!"

She cringed, then turned around and forced a bright smile.

Her boss, Mr. Lawson, was smiling back. Glancing at his watch, he then pointed to her. "We're on, ten thirty. And boy am I impressed with your work lately."

His chirpy—yet demanding—tone stripped away the last bit of sanity Jenna was holding on to. Almost as if on cue, the whirring sound increased in pitch, and she squeezed her eyes tight, raising a hand to her left ear. All was not lost; Jenna could just tell Mr. Lawson she needed to grab a quick bite before their meeting started. When she reopened her eyes, she looked behind her and caught sight of Melanie, who was already at the end of the hallway. Turning right, Melanie disappeared from sight.

Fuck!

Jenna swiveled around, bumping into Mr. Lawson. He stepped back, a baffled expression on his face, and lifted his hands up in a conciliatory manner. Shrugging, she flashed a beaming smile to overcompensate for her absolute sky-high anxiety. Her body began to tremble. Had she drunk too much coffee this morning? Had her breakfast been too small? Did she drink enough water? Before she could consider her response, her mouth blurted out the answer.

"Yes, of course!"

A stiff smile chiseled itself across Mr. Lawson's face, and with an excited pump of his fist, he tipped a curt nod. He was rigid, old-fashioned masculine energy—complete with a 70s-era Burt Reynolds mustache. "Let's get to it, then."

As Jenna walked into Mr. Lawson's office, he closed the door and motioned for her to sit opposite him at his desk. She stared at the same chair she had sat in two years ago, when she'd been promoted to a bookkeeper. That fleeting memory danced in her mind, making her wish she felt as elated now as she did then. Had she just been fooling herself this whole time? Was she really ready for this extra responsibility? Balling her hands into fists, she relished the tension, then opened her palms and enjoyed the release.

She could do this. Hell, it would only last an hour at most. Plus, he said he'd been impressed with her work. What could go wrong? Settling into this newfound perseverance, Jenna sat down on the chair, leaning forward and lacing her fingers together between her thighs.

Mr. Lawson adjusted his dress pants before sitting in his chair, cleared his throat, and placed his hand on the mouse. With a few clicks, he smiled.

"Ah, here it is. The presentation you sent me. You didn't have to *do* this, you know. But it's impressive, and I love the panache."

Jenna forced a smile and pressed her thighs together. Straightening her back, she stiffened her posture.

The incessant whirring had grown to the grating sound of buzzing mosquitoes. She imagined a mass of mosquitos packed into her Eustachian tubes, clogging up the ducts. They were smashed together—heaps of heads, thoraxes, and abdomens—squirming their spindly legs against the soft tissue and buzzing their wings, dying a slow death inside her ear cavities. She frowned and held back a dry retch.

Mr. Lawson tilted his head and pouted. "You okay, Jenna? Look like you're gonna be sick?"

Jenna fidgeted with her ear, furrowing her brow as she looked at the gray nylon carpet. All she could think about were insects now, and the differing shades of gray spanning the office floor resembled silverfish. An immense mass of tear-drop-shaped, thrashing forms. Willowy legs attached to segmented bodies scaled over each other, scuttering along in a heap of infinite and erratic madness.

"Jenna?" Mr. Lawson spoke louder this time.

Snapping out of it, Jenna looked back up to her boss. With a quick glance at the carpet, all had returned to normal, simply a sea of tight-knit fibers.

"Yes! Yes... let's start."

His eyes grew wide with concern, and he took a deep breath in, twitching his nose. His massive mustache followed suit, moving in comical fashion. After eyeing her for a few more seconds, he tipped a brisk nod. "Okay then."

Jenna focused on her breathing as Mr. Lawson analyzed his monitor, his eyes darting to and fro. She felt slight pressure in the back of her head, right above her neck. Tipping her head forward, she lifted a hand and rubbed that area, hoping to calm the tightened sensation somehow. The whirring sound had increased to a steady ring, and for the first time, she felt truly scared and utterly vulnerable.

"Jenna," Mr. Lawson spoke. "Listen, if you're not up for this right now, we can always reschedule and—"

"But I worked so hard on that PowerPoint!" Jenna blurted out, now on the verge of tears. "I worked so hard on it, and..." She winced and hunched over when the pressure in the back of her head began to throb. "I don't *want* to reschedule."

"Hey," Mr. Lawson spoke in a soft tone now, leaning forward and placing his palms on the desktop. "This will in *no* way affect your opportunity for a promotion, okay? I know we've talked about this, and I don't want you to worry." With a quick flick of his wrist, he continued. "Hell, if you need to cut out for the day, by all means." Leaning back in his chair, he gestured to his door. "If you're comin' down with something, best rest up and get back to us in tip-top shape."

Jenna wrung her hands together, considering his words. Her mind was riddled with confusion, frustration, and fear; there was no way she could get through this meeting in her current condition. Humiliation set in, scorning her with a warm blush that seized her cheeks and spread to her sternum. She wondered if her boss was just consoling her for his own benefit—rush her out of here so as not to catch what she had. Did he really mean he'd still consider her for the promotion?

Another ache throbbed in the back of her head, and she leaned forward, wincing again at the intolerable sensation. It didn't resemble the thrum of a headache. It had more... depth. Jenna had no choice. She stood up, nodding toward Mr. Lawson.

"Thank you. I'm taking your advice. Must be coming down with something." Scratching the back of her head, she cringed. "Hit me like a *freight* train."

Mr. Lawson offered his palms as he spoke. "Sometimes they do. Nothin' a Tylenol and a nap can't fix." He waved her off. "Go on now, hopefully you'll be good as new tomorrow."

"T-thanks, Mr. Lawson. We'll reschedule?" she asked, brows upturned in concern.

"You betcha." He shot her a wink, and his phone began to ring. With a polite nod toward her, he picked up the receiver and leaned back in his chair.

"Ritchie! How you been?"

FLESHY WARMTH

Though it now inhabited complete darkness, the two sets of four eyes had been imbued with a retroreflective layer, allowing the creature to discern its snug shelter in more detail. It had begun to create the space necessary for the completion of this final phase.

Sharp fangs tore into the delicate brain tissue, injecting it with miniscule amounts of the key substance. The spongy tissue obeyed, dissolving with each calculated injection. Neurons and blood vessels succumbed to each bite, with precious synapses losing vital communication pathways.

Soon it would begin to lay the groundwork for the most beautiful act of all. Though it could never know its time was limited, biological programming rendered this stage purposeful and dutiful. It was all for a grander purpose.

Such a warm, peaceful dwelling.

MERCY

The drive home had been agonizing. The throbbing in the back of Jenna's head came and went, and for a few brief moments, her hands had twitched while turning the wheel and she'd briefly lost her grasp. What was normally a leisurely commute had transformed into a test of patience and will. The sight of her house as she turned onto her street might as well have been Disney World. She was so elated to have simply made it home without getting into an accident. What the *hell* was happening to her?

Pulling into her driveway, she shifted her cherry red Volkswagen Golf into park and shut the engine off, slamming her head back against the headrest. There was a jolt of panic as her eyes shot open and she reached for the back of her head, anticipating a painful reaction to the impact. But there was nothing.

Jenna's jaw fell slack in bewilderment as she realized... the ringing and throbbing had stopped. Just like that. It had persisted for at least an hour. Is this what tinnitus was like? On one minute, off the next? The human body was both brilliant and a goddamn enigma.

Closing her eyes, she welcomed the hushed silence of the cabin and the pleasant warmth of radiant sunshine spilling in through the windshield. All was quiet for once, except the charming melody of birdsong. As she opened her eyes, she gazed upon the treetops. Branches swayed with the breeze, performing a collaborative dance. It was all so calm and serene. Maybe this whole experience was a lesson in humility.

She'd spent most waking moments degrading herself with negative self-talk and pushing herself to keep achieving more. And for what? For one more notch up the ladder at the sacrifice of her mental health and well-being. Didn't seem worth it. She told herself that if she didn't get that promotion, it wasn't a reflection on her as a person. She had achieved so much, and the art of thankfulness wasn't something to scoff at.

Avril Lavigne's voice blared from her purse, jilting her from daydreaming. "Why'd it all have to get this complicated?" Jenna said with a smirk, enjoying the irony of her new ringtone. Grabbing her Motorola, she flipped it open and noticed it was Dr. Gates's office.

"Hmm," she mused. Could be good, could be bad—time to find out. She stalled with bated breath, then answered.

"Hello?"

"Hello, am I speaking with Jenna?"

"Yes, you are."

"I'm calling to let you know that we have a slot open Wednesday morning now, if you'd like to come in earlier?"

Jenna's heart leapt to her throat in excitement. The sooner the better; she'd just call in late to work.

"Yes! Thank you so much! Another lucky day, huh?"

"Pardon?" the receptionist asked, confused.

"Oh, I'm sorry. I must have spoken to someone else before. It's supposed to be a long wait to get in to see the doctor, but I called this morning and was already lucky to get an appointment for Friday."

"Oh, I see. Yes, that's very true. Well, summer vacation plans and such. Sometimes that makes for last-minute cancellations. Does ten a.m. work?"

"Ten a.m. is *perfect*," Jenna chimed.

"Great, see you then! Have a good day."

"You too. Thanks!"

With fervid excitement, Jenna hugged her cell fast to her chest and scrunched her nose. After the complete train wreck this morning had been, she needed some good news. Stepping out of the car, her body felt weightless, and there was a spring to her step again. The universe had finally decided to accommodate. Waiting until the end of the week would have been doable but awfully long, and the little patience she still had was slipping through her fingers.

Walking to her front door, she turned the key and was greeted with a sweet, furry face. Nudging Ziggy with her foot, he scampered back inside.

"Why you always wanna leave me?" Jenna joked. "I give you food, fresh water, give you all the pets in the world, and you just wanna escape?" She walked in, closing the door behind her, and placed her purse on the hallway table. "Not only that, but I clean up your shit too!" Ziggy sat on his haunches and stared up at her with those gorgeous marble eyes. Jenna cocked her head and gazed down at him, sporting a pout. "You're lucky you're so cute." Picking him up, she nestled her face into his fur and reveled in those delicious purrs. As she carried him to the kitchen, Jenna beamed.

"I'm finally gonna tackle this, then it's no more complications for me. Sorry, Avril. Your time is short."

DISTURBING THOUGHTS

Jenna decided there was no problem in milking this lucky circumstance as it was and called in sick on Tuesday as well. This gave her even more time to prepare for her performance review with Mr. Lawson. Plus, he'd emailed her stating they could reschedule for Wednesday anyway. What was the harm in playing hooky for a bit and returning back to work bright-eyed and bushy-tailed?

She knew Mr. Lawson was deciding on the candidate by Friday, since Stephanie was leaving in two weeks.

Having been a bookkeeper for a couple years now, Jenna had finally decided she wanted to move up in the company. When Stephanie, one of the accountants, announced her departure, this was the perfect chance. Of course, Jenna was not a shoo-in. She had competition to deal with, and that competition was practically bulletproof. But she'd really gone above and beyond these past few months, and that pay raise was hers to snag.

A pay raise meant she could make more of a dent in her student loans, and it meant she could maybe even afford a better place. But above all else, it meant she could hold the promotion over her competition's head—and that felt the very best of all.

She was going up against her coworker Ben for the promotion and had to admit jealousy was part of the reason she was pushing so hard for this. Jealousy and the innate need to prove herself.

Ben was Hollywood pretty, and all the ladies in the office swooned over him, except for Jenna. He was born with a Brad Pitt jawline and impressive physique. People like him didn't have to even try; they just got by on their looks and good graces. Though Jenna was no ugly duckling, she didn't consider herself a natural beauty either.

Her eyes were too far apart, she was a bit tall and lanky, and her feet were huge. She wore size ten shoes, for goodness' sake. Plus, her stomach was perpetually distended. Sometimes she fantasized there was an inflated balloon lodged right under her ribs. She could just stick a needle into her belly, and, *hiss...* it would slowly deflate, giving her the flat stomach she had always hoped for. But at least her chubs made Ziggy happy; he'd made work of them with some mean kneading sessions.

Jenna's mind wandered back to the string of mucus she'd pulled from her eye the other day. It *had* to be mucus, right? Leaning against the kitchen counter, she placed her fingers to her lips and crossed an arm over her stomach. That thought seeped into her mind again, and she just needed to know the answer. Was such a thing *possible*? In all honesty, she had no clue. It very well could have been, and she was just blissfully unaware. If this was the case, then wasn't everyone?

Walking to the cabinet, she removed a bag of coffee grinds and a paper filter and prepped the coffee maker. A couple cups would do. No? Maybe three cups, just for good measure.

As the water reached optimum temperature and began to trickle over the grounds, she walked over to the kitchen table, where her laptop lay. Opening it, she pressed the power button and waited for the computer to boot up. When the startup sound sang and the monitor came to life, she logged in.

Pursing her lips, her fingers hovered over the keyboard. When the coffee maker began to sputter, signaling the completion of liquid caffeine, she rose and grabbed a mug from the cabinet, deciding she needed this small comfort before continuing. With a splash of milk and a dash of honey, her coffee was ready for the task at hand. Taking a sip, she smiled. *Perfect.*

Walking back to the table, Jenna sat down again with her coffee mug. After taking another sip, she began typing the question that made her skin crawl to even think about, those nasty little words she was bringing to life now. Would this give them more power? Would this make the potentially impossible possible?

Can spiders—

The phone in the kitchen trilled, announcing the caller's name. *Mom... Dammit, it's been too long. Gotta answer.* Huffing out frustration and relief—what was she even *thinking*, searching this?—Jenna stood and walked over to the phone, grabbing it from the cradle.

"Hey, Mom," she said as she trudged over to the couch and plopped down. Ziggy saw his opportunity and jumped onto her lap.

"Hi, hun. Haven't heard from you in a few days. Everything okay?"

"Yeah, everything's okay. Just been a little sick is all," she lied through her teeth.

"Oh, I'm sorry to hear. But you don't really sound sick?" Always trying to call Jenna's bluff, though she was right this time. "Maybe from your trip? I swear, you really scared me taking that trip all by yourself."

"Well, you and Dad didn't want to come with, so... figured you only live once, ya know?"

There was silence on the other end of the line, and she could hear her mom fidgeting. Resentment fizzled hot in Jenna's chest again, and the feeling of abandonment clawed at her psyche.

"How's *Mike* doing? And how are the kids?"

"Oh, they're doing great. You know, you really should make time to visit us. I know you like going on your big adventures, but you're missing your nieces and nephews grow up." Her mom sighed. "We all miss you, too."

Jenna puckered her lips in frustration. Looking down at Ziggy, she ran her fingers through his thick fur to calm herself. The nerve of this woman. "You do know that you and Dad left *me*, right? Since I'm not producing any grandkids for you." She paused, smiling. "How's North Carolina?"

"Oh, c'mon, dear. It's not like that. He just really needed the help, you know that."

"Well, it was his choice to move, so... shouldn't it be his problem to figure it out on his own? He is an adult, after all."

She could hear her mom's frustration on the other end of the line through an exasperated sigh. *Good*, she was getting under her skin. They'd always spoiled her younger brother. And she and Mike couldn't be more different. He had moved for his wife, whose relocation meant a massive raise for her big pharma job. Meanwhile, Jenna was kickin' ass all on her own.

"How's that promotion going?" her mom asked.

A pang of guilt gripped Jenna's chest, and her pent-up tension released as she sank more into the couch. "I'm sorry. It's just... I miss you guys, too. And you know me. No offense, but I do kinda like my own space." She flinched, though this wasn't a lie. "You're still visiting this fall though, right?"

"We are, and it's okay. You always did have an independent streak. But you didn't answer my question. How's that—"

"Oh yeah, yeah, yeah. That promotion. Well, as it turns out, I was able to reschedule my meeting to tomorrow. I got good hopes about this one. You didn't raise no sissy."

"I certainly did not!" Her mom's voice gushed motherly pride.

Jenna considered mentioning her tinnitus to her mom, but that would mean appearing weak, and she'd rather keep up this strong front. Also, no use in making a big fuss out of nothing. She'd be getting it squared away tomorrow.

They both sat in silence for a few seconds, neither knowing what to say. Their relationship had always been a bit rocky. Jenna had never really needed her mother's support as much as Mike had, which she felt had thrown a wrench in things. She and her dad got along well enough.

"Well, I guess I'll let you know by Friday about the promotion. It'll be decided by then."

"Sounds good, dear. And hey... don't be a stranger. I know the weather in Ohio can teeter-totter, but it's always beautiful down here."

Jenna rolled her eyes and smirked. "I'll call you soon, okay? Love you."

"Love you too, talk soon."

With that, Jenna hung up, thankful to have this obligatory conversation done with. Her mom was right, though; Jenna hadn't checked in for a while. She'd been... occupied. That last word didn't sit well with her, and she cringed, glancing at her laptop.

With renewed determination, she shot up from the couch—apologizing to Ziggy as he jumped to the floor—and stomped over to her laptop. Logging in again, Jenna finished typing those ugly, revolting words in the search box. She just needed to get them out, as ridiculous as they were. It was a primitive, primal urge to satiate:

Can spiders crawl into your brain?

Glancing over the first search result, she closed her eyes and sighed out the heaviness that had weighed on her these past few days.

No insects or arachnids are capable of entering your brain.

THE DOCTOR IS IN

The drive to Dr. Gates's office the next morning was… interesting. In fact, the entire morning had been. Jenna wasn't quite sure what was going on, but the tinnitus had paled in comparison to what it had been before. She'd felt a slight ringing when she woke up, but this had subsided. And thankfully the achiness was gone as well. She should have figured everything was too good to be true. Wasn't it always? No good reason to cling on to false hope.

Jenna thought she'd be out of the woods soon, but now a more *serious* issue had arisen. She had experienced a couple worrisome bouts of vertigo and was finding it difficult to accomplish simple tasks in a normal manner.

For instance, pulling on her jeans this morning had felt cumbersome. Her body knew what to do, but it had taken sheer concentration and will to pull it off. Pulling on a pair of *jeans* for Christ's sake. It was almost as if she had been moving in slow motion. The neurons just weren't firing properly. What kind of doctor even dealt with this? Oh yes, a neurologist. But when would she have time for that? And how the hell would she find a good one? Closing her eyes, she sighed and focused on calming her anxious mind. That lasted for a couple seconds.

Had the chicken she cooked last night gone bad? It had been in the fridge for a few days. Did she have food poisoning?

Get a grip. You're losing control.

Jenna sat in the chair in the waiting room, tapping her heels on the floor. When she noticed a middle-aged couple eyeing her with disdain, she stopped. Hunching her shoulders, she drew a deep breath in, exhaling loud enough for them to hear. Then she started to tap her heels again, more aggressive this time. The woman shot her a cold glare, and Jenna returned it, amplifying the expression. *You wanna play? Let's go, bitch.* The lady rolled her eyes and crossed her legs, getting back to reading an issue of *People* magazine. Jenna smirked in return, reveling in the fact she had stared the lady into submission. Small wins felt that much more rewarding lately.

She glanced at the clock on the wall: eleven o'clock already? Why were doctors always so famously late? Was it a code they had to adhere to? A faint buzzing sound began in Jenna's ear again, and she adjusted her posture, resting her elbow on the chair arm and leaning her cheek against her fingers. *Please don't get louder, please don't get louder, please don't—*

"Jenna?"

Jenna looked up to see a young woman standing in the doorway. Her curly black hair was pulled up into a loose bun, with wavy tendrils gracing the sides of her face. She had large, kind brown eyes and held a clipboard in her arms.

Jenna stood up and was overcome by a bout of vertigo again. Leaning over, she rested one hand on the chair arm and placed the other to her chest, seeking to regain her composure. The room was spinning, and she squeezed her eyes shut to dull the reeling sensation. When stability returned, she shot her eyes back open, noticing the young woman hurrying her way. Jenna raised her palm, and the woman slowed her advance.

"I'm fine," Jenna replied. "Just a little vertigo, probably a side effect of the tinnitus."

"Well, it can definitely cause that," the young woman answered, her words laced with concern. She gestured toward the doorway. "Follow me."

As Jenna walked to the doorway, she glanced at the middle-aged couple in the waiting room. The woman shot her an incredulous look, apparently in disbelief she hadn't been called in. Jenna simply winked at her before disappearing into the hallway, a gesture that caused the woman to scoff and knit her brow. Radiating smug satisfaction felt good, and Jenna wore it better than ever now—take control, hide the hurt.

The hallway walls were painted a muted pastel yellow, as was customary for many medical offices. A hue chosen to offset the jitters, Jenna supposed, though for her it only magnified them. A false sense of security when you're facing uncertainty. Brilliant.

She followed the young woman to the second to the last door on the left, noting the dark humor of the location. Dodged a bullet there.

"Please, sit." The young woman motioned to the examination table covered with medical exam paper, and Jenna scooted onto it. The paper always amused her. Did it offer any benefit at all other than being crinkly and brash?

Jenna was asked the reason for her visit, and she obediently answered, knowing she would have to repeat it all over again when the doctor came in. Typing the information into a laptop on a rolling desk, the young woman nodded as the keys tip-tapped in a soothing rhythm.

"Great," the young woman said when she had finished. Smacking her thighs with her hands, she then stood up. "The doctor will be in to see you." Tipping her head in an emphatic manner, she added, "I hope you feel better soon." With that, she waltzed to the door, bidding Jenna farewell with a warm smile as she closed it behind her.

Jenna was left alone to wait; not even the noises in her head decided to keep her company.

But there was the disconcerting feeling of a slight wriggle deep inside her head.

COLORFUL DR. GATES

Dr. Gates burst into the office with a bright smile and insufferable energy. He wore a navy-blue, button-up top with a tie featuring cats clad in vintage clothing reading books. Jenna opened her mouth to greet him, but she wasn't quite sure what to say. Did she address the cats on his tie, or did she wave and say hello?

Owing to exhaustion and bafflement, she chose neither, more than happy for him to take the lead. A shimmering wave of relief washed over her, knowing she could finally unload all of this baggage onto a professional who really understood and could quell her nerve-wracking fears.

He leaned forward, still beaming, and reached out his hand. When she reciprocated, he squeezed her hand firm and gave it a brisk shake.

"Jenna! Nice to meet ya. So you've been experiencing some tinnitus, huh?"

She couldn't avert her gaze from his ridiculously cute tie, which he immediately addressed. Tilting his head, he lifted the end of it with his fingers, looking upon it with admiration.

"Oh, this thing? Yeah, my daughters get a kick out of it. What can I say... It's a great icebreaker, and I love cats and books. Here, he's my favorite." He pointed to a white, fluffy cat wearing a monocle and sporting a multi-colored sweater vest and gray trousers. It was reading a green book and drinking a cup of cocoa.

"Well," Jenna chuckled. "It certainly is a good icebreaker, and I can imagine how your daughters must love it. Oh, and I have a cat too—a black cat named Ziggy." She paused, then continued, "Not much of a reader myself, but I do watch a lot of shows."

"Lots of good shows. *Dexter* is one of my favorites right now, second season is coming out this fall."

"Oh, I love *Dexter*!"

He pointed at her and clicked his tongue. "Based on a book series."

Jenna grinned. "Seems like I might have some books to read after all."

Dr. Gates clapped his hands together, both acknowledging her comment and signaling the need to move on. "But the *real* reason you're here is to talk about your tinnitus, so let's get right to it. Tell me, when did this start?"

"Mm, it started just a few days ago. Saturday."

He rubbed his hands together, anxious to get to the issue at hand. "*Saturday.* Oh, so you got in here pretty fast!"

"I did! Got lucky, I guess."

"Yes! That's good. Happy they got you in here so soon." He leaned forward, placing an elbow on his thigh and resting his chin on his fingertips. "Okay, so Saturday." Sitting up straight, he then crossed his legs and clasped his knee with his hands. He radiated effervescent energy. "Tell me, what does it sound like? Is it loud? Soft? And how long does it last?"

"Well, that's the crazy thing. It first started when I was having lunch with my friends on Saturday. Just a light ringing, ya know? And it got pretty loud, then went away. After that, it's just kinda been off and on. But sometimes..." She trailed off, hunching over and resting her forearms on her thighs. Visions of her meeting with Mr. Lawson on Monday appeared in her mind, and she shot straight up. "Oh my God, but Monday! It was *horrible*! The ringing was so loud, and I even started to get an ache in the back of my head. Just outta nowhere. It was hard to concentrate, and now all of a sudden, I find myself kinda off balance at times."

His smile faded with the delivery of this information, causing Jenna's heartbeat to quicken. *Oh, shit. That's not good.*

With a curt nod, he clapped his hands again. What was it with clapping his hands? He scooted on his swivel chair to a desk against the opposite wall with all manner of medical equipment. Picking up an otoscope, he scooted back to her, then stood up.

"Okay. Before we go any further, let's check out your ears." Tapping the otoscope, he continued, "I'm just gonna use this little guy to make sure there's no infection going on, nothing stuck in there... let's have a look-see."

Jenna pursed her lips and smiled, sitting up straighter and keeping still. She knew the drill.

There was a tickle as he evaluated each of her ears, and the plastic was cold against her skin. She listened to the sound of his breathing and his muffled steps on the linoleum floor. It was so quiet you could hear a pin drop. Such an oddly intimate moment between doctor and patient. He *was* kinda cute.

When he'd finished, Dr. Gates placed the otoscope back on the desk and sat on his swivel chair. Looking up at her, he shrugged and flashed that bright smile again. "So I do see some swelling in your left ear and a slight perforation. It's not major, but an antibiotic should wipe that out."

Jenna forced a crooked smile. "Well... I guess that's good, right? Could that be why I'm having this *ringing*?"

"Oh, absolutely! Have you traveled anywhere recently, by plane?"

"I *did*, actually. Just got back from Finland a couple weeks ago."

"Finland!" he proclaimed. "Wow! That's quite a trip. What brought you over there?"

"My aunt and uncle moved there a few years ago. They always said I'm more than welcome to visit, and... well, I decided I'd just do it! It's nice there this time of year. Got pretty chilly at night but I kept the windows open, let the cool breeze in. Their house was a bit stuffy."

"Yes, that does the trick. You went all by yourself?"

Jenna nodded, a proud grin spreading across her face. "All by myself."

"Wow, what an experience. I've always wanted to visit, ya know. Maybe I'll drag the fam there."

"Oh, please do. It's absolutely gorgeous! Only thing is," she laughed nervously, "if you have arachnophobia like I do, they have these crazy huge spiders. They're *literally* called giant house spiders. And they kinda, you know, just hang out in the house. I spotted a couple of 'em when I was there. I mean, *ew*! They're disgusting!" She wrapped her arms around herself, quelling the goosebumps that were prickling her skin.

Dr. Gates cringed and drew his arms to his chest. "Oof, those do sound scary. But, fun fact, believe it or not. One of my close friends is an entomologist. I've learned a lot about these creepy critters through her and"—he shrugged—"they're perfectly designed by nature. I mean, when you think about it: those legs, that flexibility and speed, the ability to make webs? Pretty cool, really."

Jenna shuddered, rubbing her arms. "I'm sorry, but... Shouldn't even be a thing. Just, *nope*."

Dr. Gates leaned back and laughed, slapping his knee. "Thank goodness we don't have those *here*, right? Well, come to think of it..." He touched a pointer finger to his chin. "We do have funnel-web spiders, but they're not dangerous. Oh, and, well... sorry to burst your bubble, but I think there's some huntsman down south." With a wave of his hand, he said, "But hey, we're in Ohio. What do we have here—common house spiders, right?"

"I suppose," Jenna said. Her skin had been crawling during this entire conversation, and she felt something move on her head. Swatting at it, she realized it was nothing at all. Just her lovely imagination.

Dr. Gates noticed her discomfort and tilted his head, smiling soft and warm. "Why don't we take a detour from talking about the creepy-crawlies and get back to why I asked you that." Crossing his arms and legs, he continued.

"It's very common to get tinnitus after air travel, and, though it's rare, you can rupture your eardrum too. The pressure changes can knock everything outta whack, and this of course affects the regulation of your Eustachian tube." He moved his hands in a wheel-like motion as he spoke. "I'm surprised you haven't had much pain, and, though this could resolve on its own, I'm going to prescribe you some ear drops and some Flonase."

"*Flonase?*" Jenna asked, confused.

"Yes," he chuckled. "I get this response a lot. Flonase helps with inflammation, so it can be a Band-Aid—if you will—while this resolves itself."

Jenna took a big inhale of relief, and exhaled a heavy dose of worry. "So you don't think this is that serious?"

"I don't," he replied. "And vertigo can be a common occurrence along with this, owing to how the inner ear regulates balance. But I *do* want to see you back here in two weeks. If this hasn't resolved by then, we'll move on to Plan B."

"Which is?" She cringed, waiting for his response.

"Just some testing," he answered. "But,"—he placed his palm to his chest—"I have a good feeling this will go away."

Jenna kicked her feet back and forth in blissful glee. For the first time, there was finally a silver lining.

A horrific thought burst into her mind as the memory of that mucus string surfaced, but she abruptly dismissed it... just wasn't possible.

FIERCE DETERMINATION

Jenna left the doctor's office feeling lighter, freer, *hopeful*. She reached her car and opened the door, plopping into the driver's seat. Closing the door, she set her purse on the passenger seat, then fished out her phone and navigated to Lisa's contact. In quick succession, she typed her message in, elated to deliver the good news. Lisa should hear it first, since she gave Jenna this lead on Dr. Gates. Placing her phone back in her purse, she smiled and started up the engine.

Her phone chimed almost immediately, and she picked it up, eager to view Lisa's reply: *"Told u! Don't worry. Go get ur promotion!"*

"Don't mind if I do," Jenna said as she typed out her reply to Lisa: *"Thx so much! I'm on it. Love u!"*

Jenna opened the moonroof, allowing the brilliant morning sunshine to spill in, and headed to the office. With Mr. Lawson being able to reschedule her performance review for today (the universe really was working in her favor), her life was beginning to fall into place again. She'd secure this promotion, then pick up her medication after work, and start hitting this thing head-on now that she had newfound determination.

There was a slight buzz in her ears as she drove on, but she disregarded it. When a sharp ache took hold again, though, Jenna winced and muttered under her breath, "Motherfucker, I'm gonna starve you. You're on your way out, I'm done with this shit." She considered that *starve* was an interesting word choice, seeing as this meant something existed with which to deny sustenance. After mulling this over for a second or two, she disregarded the thought, sending it into the dark recesses of her subconscious.

Despite the ache in the back of her head turning into a throb again, Jenna drove on, resolute to plow through this ordeal. There was *no* way she was rescheduling with her boss again, come hell or high water. Relief in the form of medication was on its way, and she could endure slight discomfort in the interim.

She was fucking Jenna Taylor—voted Most Valuable Player on her high school softball team, graduated with a 4.0 GPA from Ohio State University, and just dumped her lazy-ass boyfriend because she set the bar high. This was *not* going to be what broke her.

Jenna walked into the office with her head held high, disregarding the fact that she still had intermittent aching and ringing; vertigo continued to warp her balance and sanity as well. She wasn't repeating Monday's spectacular failure all over again, though. And when it was time to meet with Mr. Lawson, Jenna put on a brave face and pushed all of her worry and doubt deep down where it belonged. In magnificent fashion, she conveyed with unwavering certainty why she was the best person for this position. If she was up for an Oscar, then by God she'd be in good standing—what an act.

For all of her perceived shortcomings, she did receive compliments. People fawned over her light blue eyes—described them as the color of ice—in contrast with her raven hair. And she did have beautiful, long fingers. Her friends used to say she could be a hand model. Maybe that was an avenue she should have pursued. Of course, that didn't require much talent. What were the accolades in that? Easy money, she supposed.

What Ben had that she lacked in spades, however, was natural charisma. He could walk into a room and immediately the vibe would shift. Ben had this uncanny calming effect on people and was able to deliver critical feedback while cushioning the blow. He'd perfected the art of the compliment sandwich, a technique she struggled with. And his voice... smooth like butter. Hers could be a bit shrill, and she had a hard time speaking slowly. So many thoughts always wanted to be verbalized, competing with each other for first pick.

How *did* people manage to speak slowly and with purpose? And yet, this wasn't an issue with confidence. Some liked to say low self-confidence spurred erratic speech, but she *was* confident; maybe a bit entitled, but who wasn't?

Looking at the clock display on her desktop, she noticed it was 4:45. Time to call it a day and swing by Walgreens to pick up her medication.

On her way out, she passed Ben, who flashed her that bright smile gleaming flawlessly white. Sure, she'd give him the honor of noticing him. Tilting her head, she shot him a wink and planned to hustle by. No time for pleasantries.

When a bout of vertigo seized her again, she hurled forward. Strong arms caught her fall, and Jenna was left hovering over the nylon carpet, just inches from her face. A dizzying sensation washed over her as she was positioned upright, still a bit delirious. Turning around, she faced Ben, who still had a strong arm wrapped around her waist.

"Whoa! You okay, Jenna?" That smooth voice again, but she wasn't falling for the fake sincerity.

"I-I'm fine, thanks."

She slowly removed his arm from her waist and took a deep breath in, sighing in frustration. "Good luck."

Ben's eyes squinted in confusion and his mouth quivered, completely stumped. Was this not important to him? Surely, he had to know she was referring to the promotion.

With a frustrated smirk, Jenna turned around and headed out. No time for an explanation. Right now, all she could focus on was how much this goddamn condition was hijacking her life.

As if on cue, she felt a squirm flutter in the depths of her head.

SPIDER LEG

The line at the Walgreens pharmacy was long, and Jenna's patience was growing ever shorter. A few people chose to rattle off their entire day to the pharmacy clerk, to which he politely nodded and continued to scan. He couldn't care less.

Just pay for it, thank the cashier, and move the fuck on. Not that hard!

Ear drops were no biggie, but Jenna did find Flonase a bit daunting. She had never inhaled anything through her nose before, and it didn't sound especially pleasant. Would she do it right? She supposed any amount of the spray would help, whether she got a full dose in or not.

Looking ahead of her, Jenna noticed only two people in line now. *Thank God.* She was barely holding it together and just wanted to get to the safety of her quiet place and administer these meds. Her muscles were so taut you could bounce a penny off of them. She began tapping the sole of her flat on the floor; anything to keep it together. Being tall, she rarely wore heels, even kitten heels. Her fight-or-flight response had kicked into high gear, resulting in perspiration.

Observing her clammy palms, she noticed the fine layer of moisture glistening under the hazy glow from the LED lights above. Rubbing her palms on her dress pants, she puffed her cheeks and stayed the course. People just weren't her thing; more specifically, crowds weren't her thing. She could feel everyone's steely eyes on her, scrutinizing each single move.

The last person in front of her, an elderly lady, left the line. Relief washed over Jenna in shimmering waves and, with gusto, she approached the counter. Placing her purse on the countertop, she requested her medications. With a few clicks of the keyboard, the crinkle of a paper bag, and minimal conversation, the ear drops and Flonase were hers. Thanking the clerk, who seemed to appreciate the minimal conversation as well, she eagerly made a beeline to the front doors.

On her way out, Carla from high school was walking in, that same fake smile she'd always donned carved into her pretty little face. Why hadn't Jenna moved far away from these freaks? Carla had been homecoming queen, head cheerleader, and all manner of pompous self-importance in high school. Just your typical run-of-the-mill snob.

When she opened her mouth to deliver what would surely be slimy insincerity, Jenna sped by without a peep, bumping her hard in the shoulder. She smiled when she heard Carla whine and moan. Some people didn't understand that after high school, no one gives a fuck how cool you were. Welcome to real life, where you actually need common sense.

The drive home had been thankfully uneventful, with little traffic. When she pulled into the driveway, Jenna rushed into her duplex unit and closed the front door behind her, letting the stress slough off with a strenuous inhale and a slow and gentle exhale. Her muscles responded in kind, releasing tension and allowing her blood to flow freely again. Clutching the paper bag tight in her hands, it crinkled under her grip. *Here goes nothing.*

Walking to the kitchen, Jenna took the ear drops and Flonase out of the paper bag. Choosing the Flonase first, she read the directions and nodded with comprehension. Simple enough. The box was sealed tight, so she clawed it open, desperate for relief at this point.

Lifting the Flonase to eye level, she inspected the bottle. Interesting design. Per the instructions, she blew her nose, then shook the bottle for good measure before administration. Then, removing the green cap, she tilted her head forward. Was this gonna hurt? If it did, she'd survive. Pushing down on the white nozzle, she sprayed the mist into her right nostril. Hmm, not that bad. Switching to her left nostril, she repeated.

There was a tickle in her throat, and she instinctively coughed—a rush of air escaping from her nostrils as well. She'd been holding the Kleenex close to her nose and noticed something black strewn on the white tissue. Something black and... sinewy.

What the fuck?

Walking to the window, Jenna lifted the tissue closer to her line of sight and analyzed this strange object in more detail. The soft, warm golden hour sunlight spilling through illuminated the tissue in a beautiful sheen, yet the black item was jarring against the silky fabric. Lifting it even closer, she realized it had segments. Sharp edges contorted into a rigid *V* shape, with one side noticeably longer than the other.

Jenna realized with absolute terror that it resembled a spider leg.

DELICATE

The sac structure had been constructed with care, beginning with the bottom ring. Then she began to weave the perimeter. Spinnerets produced a series of delicate, yet incredibly strong, strands of silk that were woven round and round in dizzying beauty. When a mistake was made, she instinctively backtracked and adjusted, then continued. Such was this architect's natural design.

When the silken pouch had been completed, she carefully deposited the cluster of translucent pearly masses into it. The batch was packed tight, with the lumpy deposit protruding against the soft, glossy lining.

She then covered the opening with much diligence, taking it upon herself to ensure complete concealment. When her masterpiece was finally completed, she rested.

And she waited.

DARK SPIRAL

Time stood still, and Jenna's peripheral vision dimmed to a dark haze. All she could focus on was that *thing* in the center of the tissue. Her heart thumped rapidly, preparing her for fight or flight. But if the danger is *inside* of you, there's no escaping it. You're simply along for the ride... hell, you *are* the ride.

This couldn't be what she thought it was; there was just no way. The doctor was right—her recent flight must have triggered all of her symptoms. Her recent flight from Finland, where spiders the size of her palm scuttled the earth on their elongated, segmented legs.

Think, Jenna.

The sound of her shallow breathing was an afterthought. It was simply an involuntary noise, a sign that she was still alive. Walking back to the kitchen, she turned the light on and placed the tissue on the round kitchen table. Then she walked over to her purse in lethargic fashion, the walk of an inmate on death row. Grabbing her phone from her purse, Jenna accessed the camera. The ringing in her head had begun again, and this time it was piercing.

Blinking her eyes, she fought another bout of vertigo. The trembling in her limbs made it nearly impossible to take a clear shot of the black thread on the tissue. Taking a deep breath in, she braced herself and bent at the waist, leaning in closer. When she felt she had it just right, she took the shot.

Leaving the tissue on the table, Jenna sat down in one of the chairs and looked out the window at the glorious sunset painting the sky in rich hues of gold and lavender. Such beauty... beauty she hoped she would be able to witness for years to come. The weight of her phone was noticeable in her hands again, tottering in her shaky grasp. A warm tear trickled down her cheek, and her lips quivered in fear. Lowering her gaze to her phone, she zoomed in on the photo, click by sickening click. When the photo appeared large enough, she forced herself to study it. Though blurry, there were definite hard angles. It looked telescopic and spiny, and she pursed her lips as she sniffled and wiped watery snot from her nose with her wrist.

There was an immediate cold, steely jolt of fear as she quickly analyzed her wrist to make sure there were no more spiny bits coming out of her nose. Of course, what she was observing in the photo could just be dried, bloody snot. Maybe her mind was playing a sick trick on her again. Setting her phone down, she stood up and reached for the tissue. Now that she had a picture of it, she could toss it.

The object on the tissue twitched.

"Oh my God!" Jenna screamed, covering her mouth and walking backward until she bumped against the wall. She slowly slid down the hard surface into a crouching position. "No, no, no..." Shaking her head, Jenna stared at the table. This wasn't real. Then, it happened: Paralyzing fear turned into fiery rage.

"Get... the fuck... *out* of me!"

Jenna banged her head hard against the wall. Then she banged it again, and again, and again... all the while her mouth was contorted into a silent scream, yet only drawling whimpers came out. The pain in the back of her head was searing now, and, reaching with her hand, she felt warm fluid. *Yes, blood. I'll crack my head open if that's what it takes. Then you'll leave me.*

As Jenna's eyes fluttered and the searing pain in her head radiated with each impact, she smiled. This is what she should have done all along. How could she have been so stupid?

The sound of her front door being thrown open could be heard amidst the wet thud of her skull against

the unforgiving surface, and uneven footsteps shuffled her way.

ABYSMAL ARRIVAL

Jenna's body swayed with the lulling movement of the car, and she glanced out the window to see the streetlights whizzing by. They left an afterimage behind: a dreamy, wavy dark gray line that lingered in her field of vision. It made her think of musical notes... She thought of the cartoons she used to watch as a kid where chubby notes would dance over wavy lines.

A voice spoke from the front seat, panicked but with a sugary lilt. "Now don't you worry, Jenna. We're gettin' you to the hospital, you'll be in tip-top shape in no time."

It was the voice of her landlord, Mrs. Miller. In a more hushed tone, she continued. "Jesus, Roger. Whaddya think made her *do* that to herself? Good Lord, that poor *girl*!"

"Dunno, Betsy. All we gotta worry about is gettin' her to the hospital. Look in the back, she still look okay?"

A hand, soft as papier-mâché, gripped Jenna's hand. Jenna swiveled her head to see Mrs. Miller smiling and nodding.

"You're gonna be okay, sweetie," Mrs. Miller cooed. "*Lordy*, don't know what came over ya. But we'll get ya good as new."

"Z-zi..." Jenna whispered.

"Zi? Dear, I don't understand." Mrs. Miller furrowed her brows and tilted her head, pouting.

"My... my cat."

"Oh, of course!" the elderly woman chimed. "He's safe and sound, don't you worry. We'll check on him for ya."

Jenna closed her eyes and smiled. Her muddled mind was clearing, the pieces fitting together. Mr. and Mrs. Miller had found her, and they were taking her to the hospital. Ziggy was okay. Everything would be okay... but wait, her head? What about her head? She shuddered as the pain hit her in droves. Incessant, stabbing pain ignited from the back of her skull and radiated in all directions. But it was necessary, wasn't it? It was necessary to push it out.

The car veered off of the freeway onto an exit, where restaurant signs loomed high in the night sky, dotting the inky blackness with bursts of red, blue, and yellow. Their presence was welcoming: familiar logos conjuring up warm feelings of nostalgia.

As they turned right onto the main road, the hospital appeared farther down on the left. Its towering structure was ominous in the gloom, and the soft illumination of letters had a blurry underwater quality. The Millers frantically shuffled in the front seat, and Jenna could hear inaudible mumbling.

They pulled up to the emergency entrance, and Mrs. Miller stepped out and opened Jenna's door. She reached down, looping a firm arm around Jenna's back and gripping her hand. She was stronger than her older age made her look, and Jenna shifted her body's weight to the right, stepping out of the car with gentle assistance. She hunched over in pain, crying out as the instant rush of blood to her head caused an incessant and painful throbbing sensation.

Jenna was here to be proven wrong. She was here to be proved an absolute idiot. *Jenna thought she had a spider in her head. Jenna fucked herself up for nothing. Jenna this, Jenna that—*

"Stop!" Jenna screamed.

Mrs. Miller halted, staring up at Jenna with wide eyes beckoning for an answer. "I'm sorry?"

Jenna knit her brow, and her breathing became raspier and more pronounced. "It's... it's nothing."

She nodded toward the entrance, and they began their slow and careful ascent up the ramp. Mrs. Miller steadied Jenna with a firm grasp on her arm. When they reached the top, the older woman looked back to her husband and nodded. He nodded in return, then began driving to the parking garage.

As luck would have it when they walked through the emergency entrance, only four people were seated in need of emergency care. It was a Wednesday night, not notorious for being very busy.

An older couple sat next to each other in a row toward the entrance, the woman laying her head on the man's shoulder. A few rows forward, a young girl sat rocking back and forth in her seat. A woman sitting next to her, had to be her mother, was tracing gentle circles along the young girl's back. The girl turned to look at Jenna as she walked toward the counter. It was such an innocent, scrutinizing stare, something only a child could pull off without offense. To wit, Jenna crossed her eyes and stuck her tongue out. The girl giggled, her shoulders bouncing up and down. Then a cough took hold, and her fragile figure convulsed with each violent whoop.

Jenna pouted, thinking about how scared the girl must have been. She also longed for how that vulnerable innocence felt, remembering the blissful weightlessness—before life laughed in merriment, clawing it away with each sobering lesson.

The young woman at the emergency counter stood up as Jenna was escorted by her landlord. She was a petite brunette with olive skin. Wrinkling her nose, her posture stiffened and her brown eyes grew wide with concern.

As Mrs. Miller answered each of the young woman's questions, Jenna bobbed her head in a rhythmic manner. She felt it... a swarm of tickles deep in the back of her head: moving, preparing, wanting.

And that pressure. *Oh God*, that pressure. It felt as if on the precipice of bursting.

IT'S SHOWTIME

Jenna went through the motions as the triage nurse took her vitals. She was sitting in a chair, and Mrs. Miller stood next to her, beaming down with an exaggerated smile, doing her best to smooth over a visage wrought with concern. Her husband stood by her side, and Jenna could hear them whispering to each other. Something about Jenna's parents. The words "sit tight" and "not to worry" were audible, but not much else.

As the nurse asked Jenna each question, she was able to answer reasonably enough. Though her mind was swimming, she still had the wherewithal to listen and respond. A male nurse walked into the room, nodding to the triage nurse who had just finished Jenna's assessment. He looked down at Jenna and reached a hand out. Rotating her head slowly upward,

Jenna regarded Mrs. Miller with all the wonder of a child. Her landlord motioned for her to get up.

"He's going to examine your head, dear. Make sure everything's okay." As Mrs. Miller spoke those last words, she reached out to Jenna's head, then cringed. Moving her hand back to her side, she simply nodded. "You're in good hands now. We'll stay here. Don't you worry." An excited "oof" escaped her lips, and Mrs. Miller placed Jenna's purse into her lap. "Don't want to go forgetting this now, do ya?"

Jenna opened her mouth to thank her, but only a puzzled moan came out. Though she was physically here, her consciousness felt elsewhere. Living and breathing, yet she felt as though she were simply a mass of flesh and bone following instructions: a cog in an expansive medical machine. When a wheelchair was rolled into the room by another hospital employee, Jenna grabbed the male nurse's hand as he helped her up and into the chair.

It had become harder to balance, and the most mundane tasks were incredibly challenging. Lifting her hand, for instance, had taken intense concentration.

As Jenna was wheeled through the hospital, the pressure in her head continued to radiate. It felt as if her brain were becoming plasticized. She imagined the soft and delicate tissue expanding and contracting against her skull, invisible fingers fidgeting the intricate mass of neuron-infused fat. She remembered vaguely what a walnut looked like when you cracked open the shell. A tiny brain… almost felt cannibalistic chewing its smooth, creamy meat.

The friction of the wheels against the linoleum floor vibrated through the wheelchair into Jenna's body, the buzzing becoming a small comfort as she was pushed through what felt like a never-ending maze of sharp corners and dizzying hallways. When the wheelchair finally came to a stop in front of the open door of a room, she peeked in and recognized the MRI machine.

She'd had an MRI once before in her twenties, when an untreated UTI had traveled to her kidneys.

"We've reached our destination," the male nurse said from behind her as he locked the wheels. His voice was so sweet, and she guessed it matched his face when he walked in front of her. Quickly scanning her to confirm the absence of jewelry, he nodded and muttered a pleased "mm-hmm," then reached his hand out again to help her up. He had curly brown hair and hazel eyes that sparkled over adorable dimples.

Smiling, Jenna clutched her purse with one hand as she accepted his gentle grasp with the other. He led her to the changing room, where she was instructed to remove her clothing and any jewelry, then don one of those drab hospital gowns. She never wore jewelry, so had none to remove. These gowns always made her feel so exposed and vulnerable, and in her current condition she felt aged well beyond her years. The brain fog and lethargy alone triggered a sense of utter helplessness.

A technician was standing at a counter on the side of the MRI room, busying herself with paperwork. When the tech heard Jenna escorted in by the nurse, she turned around and flashed a bright smile. Her kind, green eyes popped against her ivory skin and black hair. Streaks of gray adorned her ebony tresses, giving her a sage appearance.

"Well, my dear," the tech spoke. "Let's see what's going on in that head of yours, get you all fixed up." Noticing Jenna's aloofness, she continued, "Have you had an MRI before?"

Yes. The word sounded off. When the tech tilted her head and gave a look of concern, Jenna realized she hadn't spoken the word out loud. "Yes," she asserted with as much confidence as she could muster.

The tech softly placed her hands together in a prayer gesture. "Great, so you know the drill. And, well... if you're claustrophobic, just take relaxed breaths—in and out. Hate to break it to ya, but this will last about thirty minutes." She paused, then raised a hand, signifying her next line of thought. "As you know, there will be a loud clicking—almost like a jackhammer, I've heard some say."

Lady, you have no fucking clue.

"Yes," Jenna replied with a strained smile. She walked over to the machine with exerted effort, as if she were submerged in water and pushing against dense resistance. The machine sat before her, appearing futuristic in its design, a portal to another dimension. If she closed her eyes, would she be taken away from here? It was such a lovely thought, the ability to escape this prison her own body had become. She could do thirty minutes; in her groggy state, she could lay there for an hour or more.

The tech handed her a pair of foam earplugs. "For your safety. Gotta protect that hearing."

Willing her fingers to open, Jenna took the earplugs from the woman's palm, then slowly nestled them in her ears. She could tell by the tech's furrowed brow and twisted mouth that she was concerned but paid it no mind. The last thing she wanted now was sympathy. She just wanted to get this over with... though that meant getting an answer.

Jenna wasn't sure she really wanted to know what was happening inside her skull.

HATCHING

The initial stage had progressed nicely, as was expected. Translucent larvae underwent their first molt, and the egg sac in turn clouded in color to a dusky black. This molt allowed for more movement, and hundreds of minute, thread-like legs stretched and bent within their delicate yolk casings. And when the hatching began, oh what a wondrous sight.

Miniscule fangs resembling talons opened and closed in a fervor as each spiderling maneuvered within the carefully woven dwelling. On cue, their mother began to gently tear into her silken masterpiece. Just as instinct had determined its construction, instinct also deter-mined the imminent freedom of her babies.

Mother Nature played out beautifully, a calculation of careful execution.

HEAD CASE

As her head was carefully situated within the ring of the MRI machine, Jenna welcomed this brief respite. She didn't have to think, didn't have to make any decisions, didn't have to utilize any mental energy whatsoever. It was absolute bliss. Closing her eyes, she allowed her body to relax, and her mind followed suit.

"Okay, dear," she heard the tech say over the microphone from the control room. "I'm going to begin, just make sure to remain completely still during the scan."

Jenna took a deep breath in, letting out a slow and controlled *whoosh* as she emptied the air from her lungs. The calibration began, and booming sounds blared from the machine. Forget a jackhammer... it sounded like a goddamn jet engine. As if in response to this stimulus, she felt *movement* in her head again:

squirming. Chalking this up to her active imagination, she took a few deep breaths in, positive it would cease. Just a case of nerves, nothing more.

But it continued.

The sensation felt as if tiny feathers were tickling along the deep grooves of her spongy brain tissue, navigating the crevices between the fatty folds.

The image in her mind now was sickening: small, spindly black spots skittering within the tight folds of her brain beneath the webbed membrane, barely visible under the translucent and delicate meshing and—

"OH MY GOD!"

The MRI tech's harrowing scream was audible from within the enclosed room she sat in. It was followed by gagging sounds, then the indistinguishable wet gush of retching. In haste, the tech stumbled out of the room. Jenna's eyes darted all around her, yet her body stayed frozen in fear. What the *hell* was going on?

Against protocol, she utilized the scant space she had within the machine's ring to lift her head slightly and peered at the tech. For a few terrifying seconds, they locked eyes. The tech's expression was that of absolute disgust, and her mouth contorted so sharply it appeared as if her face would collapse into itself: the appearance of shriveled fruit.

Pointing at Jenna, the tech covered her mouth with her other hand. Her arm shook as she struggled to steady herself. Eyes that were calm and certain just moments ago now flared with absolute terror.

"You have..." she sputtered. "You somehow have..." Vomit seeped between the tech's fingers as she clutched her mouth, and she keeled over again, her body convulsing with each retch. Wet chunks of hurl splattered against the linoleum floor; the sickening, pulpy splash resonated within the silence of the room. Then the tech flung open the door to the MRI room, her entire body swinging in motion as she did so, and lunged into the hallway.

Jenna lay on the scanner bed, blinking her eyes in quick succession. Her heartbeat thundered in her temples now, and the pain in her head throbbed hot with each surge of blood pumping through her brain. She wiggled her fingers, body frozen in place yet buzzing with the surge of frenetic energy bubbling inside her. As the MRI machine began to produce that booming sound again, Jenna wiggled herself out and placed her feet on the floor, staring at the control room containing the monitors on which the scans were displayed.

The machine droned behind her as she trudged toward the control room, seemingly protesting her exit. Gripping the side of the door, she stepped into the small room, noticing the blue and white light emitted from the monitor screens.

Jenna directed her attention to the monitor displaying her brain scan as she removed the earplugs from her ears.

The pungent, sweet smell of vomit assailed her nostrils, and she covered her nose and mouth, fighting the need to purge herself. Greenish-yellow spew covered the front of the desk the computers sat on, trailing outside of the room. She grimaced, blinking in a forceful manner as she stepped closer to the table.

Leaning forward, she squinted her eyes, inspecting the image. There was definitely something noticeable in the back of her brain. Subconsciously rubbing the back of her head now, she analyzed the image in more detail.

It was large and round—cyst-like with a lumpy contour. But instead of appearing pitch black, a white, feathery texture was visible as a thin sheath covering what was inside. Several threadlike strings made up this sheath, spanning the circumference of the mass. And beneath it, a myriad of circular septations were visible. They were all lodged closely together, an innumerable number filling the entire space within. But some retained more definition than others, revealing small shapes with sinewy appendages.

An object could be seen along the periphery of the cyst-like mass—oval in shape with needle-like and jointed appendages. It seemed to be protecting what was inside, guarding it, making sure that... The repulsive realization of what Jenna was looking at dawned on her, and hot acid shot up her throat.

She had a spider egg sac developing in her brain.

INFESTATION

Steamy purge splattered to the floor as Jenna's body snapped forward at the hip. She struggled to breathe with each whiplash retch, one hand placed on the table and the other on her stomach. A layer of wet, chunky spew covered her arm. When reprieve finally came and she was able to draw in some deep breaths, Jenna remained hunched over, staring into nothingness; damp spittle clung to her chin and foamy saliva dripped from her lower lip onto the splatter of hurl below.

In this very moment, a brief thought offered warmth from the prickling fear—how wonderful dissolution would feel... to be able to simply disappear. No more pain, no more false hope, just sweet nothingness.

But it wasn't meant to be.

She was an utter abomination right now, at the mercy of an arachnid that had burrowed into her brain somehow and was using her spongy, warm tissue as a breeding ground. She was the literal embodiment of life imitating art. People like to say, "make it make sense." Brain-eating bacteria? That made horrifying sense. A brain-eating spider? How the *fuck* did that make sense?

Jenna thought of her internet search the other day: *No, spiders cannot crawl into your brain.* This defied all logic. And arachnophobia? Hell, let's shoot that up one, two... a trillion notches! Yet, she couldn't escape it this time because it was nestled in her goddamn *brain*, eating away at that central processor responsible for living and breathing existence.

How long can you survive without your brain function? But isn't it really your brain stem that renders you functional? That vital structure that ran parallel to the egg sac now nestled in her brain? So close together, so... Jenna blinked as she regained her composure.

She was in the hospital. She had a developing spider egg sac in her brain. She had to—

Looking around the control room, she couldn't spy the object she had in mind. She needed to get out of here; time to end this right now.

Lurching forward, Jenna made her way to the changing room. She knew well enough her phone was in her purse. Did she really need it right now? Maybe. Depended on how this all played out. When she'd draped the long strap of her purse over her shoulder, she reached the entrance to the hallway and glanced to her left and right. It was nearly empty, save for two people dressed in scrubs at the far end.

With excessive effort, she stepped out into the hallway, falling against her back on the far wall. Placing her palms on the hard surface for stability, she closed her eyes and regained her composure. Turning her body, she willed herself to place one heavy foot in front of the other and began to walk with one hand pressed against the wall for leverage. But she wasn't really walking, was she? She thought of herself as a zombie, a hideous creature: an abomination.

As she reached the end of the hallway, she looked to her left and right again. Immense pressure flared in her head now, and Jenna knew what it was. She knew with absolute, terrifying certainty what it was. Momma had picked a hospitable place for her young ones; Momma had done good. Nothing could infiltrate that egg sac... except Jenna was already one step ahead.

You need me, Momma? Well, tough shit. I'm ending you!

An elevator was situated to her right. She swung around to face it, supporting her weight with a firm hand placed against the wall, and pushed the button. Was that the up button or the down button? Did it matter? The door opened and a petite woman glared at Jenna, scoffing as she exited. Jenna's head slowly pivoted on her neck, following the lady's departure, hoping to instill fright. *I'm a freak. Welcome to the freak show!*

The lady glanced back at Jenna as she walked on, and a flicker of fear sparked in her expression. There it was... The lady's head snapped forward and her steps quickened, heels clacking in a brisk stride against the linoleum floor.

Plodding into the elevator, Jenna shook her head and leaned back against the wall, catching her breath. She wasn't sure where she was going, but she damn well knew what she needed to find was somewhere in this building. A couple buttons were lit up, so she allowed the elevator doors to close and took her chances. The throbbing in her head continued, and she imagined her entire brain pulsating: a spongy mass that had been desecrated. Tiny pincers and spindly legs were breaking through the web-like mesh of membrane protecting it.

Jenna closed her eyes, enjoying the soft lull of the elevator as it transported her to another floor. And when the doors opened, several patient rooms were visible. Taking her chances, she lurched to the right, leaning her side against the wall as she trudged forward with each step. A couple people in plain clothes were walking her way, a few rooms down. She could see the flash of surprise in their eyes, and their jaws dropped as they began to rush toward her, but she didn't want to be saved by them.

She would be saving herself.

Jenna noticed a nursing station to the left, donning computer monitors, phones, and all manner of medical supplies. And lucky her, the station was unoccupied. That glorious item she had been looking for was visible in an open drawer as she snaked around the corner of the desk. It glimmered, aglow with a sheen from the bleak LED ceiling lights. As she reached to grab it, her phone rang in her purse. Knitting her brow, she huffed in frustration. Did she answer out of sheer amusement or ignore this untimely distraction? Shrugging, she fished out her cell phone and flipped it open, lifting the device to her ear. Lisa's ecstatic voice trilled from the other end of the line.

"Jenna! Jenna, where are you? You got the promotion! I just heard it. You did it! I'm so proud of you!"

Jenna smiled as a warm tear trickled down her cheek. Dropping her phone, she grabbed the scissors from the drawer seconds before a pair of hands snatched her shoulders.

With all the strength she could muster, Jenna stabbed herself in the ear. The cold steel drove in obediently, puncturing her eardrum and continuing on to penetrate her skull and sever the delicate brain membranes. When it slid into her soft, spongy brain, slicing through rich, neuron-infused meat, it came in contact with her brain stem. What a fortunate angle... B ingo.

I won.

***

The couple holding Jenna's lifeless body in their arms stood there in shock, lips trembling. It had all happened so fast. They lowered her gently to the floor, and the girl immediately checked Jenna's pulse. Looking up to her boyfriend, she shook her head. He rubbed the back of his neck and winced.

"You wait here, Ally," he told her. "I'm gonna get help."

"But I don't wanna—"

"Just wait! Be back soon, I promise."

Pursing her lips, she nodded, and he ran down the hall.

Ally sat there on the floor next to the dead woman's body, fingers pressed to her lips in anxious anticipation. The woman was so beautiful, with long, black hair and the most gorgeous blue eyes. And was that a smug smile adorning her pale face? It didn't take long for Ally to notice something else... The woman's skin was pulsating around the swollen wound in her ear.

Blinking her eyes rapidly, Ally looked around to call out, but no one was there. Sick curiosity took over, and she situated herself into a crouch, reaching very slowly for the gray finger holes of the scissors that were jammed through the woman's ear.

Steeling her breath, Ally yanked the scissors out, dropping them immediately to the floor as she stood up and backed away, holding her hands up protectively in front of her. The scissors landed with a metallic clang on the linoleum floor, and blood began to gush out of the wound. Ribbons of pink cerebrospinal fluid swirled within the crimson.

Something on the scissors caught her attention; some kind of substance clung to the blades. It laced along them—scarlet-colored gossamer. She then spied several clusters of small beads donning feathery threads squirming within the pinkish-red fluid. They were *everywhere,* writhing within the thick liquid.

When a few small and slightly translucent objects skittered out of the lady's ear, scurrying over the wriggling cluster below, she realized what they were... freshly hatched spiderlings.

As Ally's pounding footsteps echoed down the hallway, dozens of spiderlings crawled their way out of the wound in Jenna's ear. Their cream-colored bodies scrambled over discolored flesh and down her cheek to the cold floor, scuttling along in search of a dark, cushy dwelling.

EPILOGUE

Hank sat in his hospital bed, brushing the few strands of wispy black hair still sprouting from his scalp to the side with his fingers. Gina would be here shortly, and he wanted to look his best given the circumstances. Doctors said he'd be out soon; the appendix removal had gone well. He admired himself in the hand mirror. She had gifted it to him before his surgery to remind him he was his greatest champion, and he'd get through this. *Who should have your back all the time? Well, take a look there in that mirror,* that's *who.*

The news was playing on the TV mounted on the wall, and a couple words caught his attention: "experiment" and "spider." Reaching for the remote, he turned the volume up and listened in. The male newscaster's face was solemn as he continued.

"It is impervious to the elements, and is presumed to have escaped across the border. We have learned that Russia has been conducting experiments on this bioengineered spider for some time as a weapon of mass destruction. It is able to penetrate through the skull and enter the brain by secreting acid, where it creates an egg sac, thereby propagating."

The newscaster then hesitated, tapping his pen on the tabletop in nervous fashion.

"The spider in question is a sac spider, a common household spider. And if this isn't concerning enough, it is said to propagate at an alarming rate. Meaning the spiderlings can hatch within days, not weeks. The females will continue reproducing, while the males will simply feast on brain tissue.

"We have reports of a concerning case in Ohio, but have been told this situation is under control and there should be no need to panic."

The newscaster looked down, shaking his head and wiping his brow. He trembled as he chuckled, sporting a nervous smile.

"Well, there you have it. Your worst nightmare imagined, come true. Good thing this is under control, because the alternative could mean absolute chaos on a global scale."

Hank stared at the TV in a catatonic state, blinking his eyes as he tried to comprehend what he just heard.

There was a tickle along the back of his neck, and he swatted at it. Clearing his throat, he looked back into the mirror. The bags under his eyes told of no sleep, but other than that his handsome mug looked pretty okay.

A milky, opaque spiderling skittered up the side of his neck and burrowed into his ear. Hank's eyes grew wide and his mouth shot open as—

A bloodcurdling scream rang out from room 396, followed by each subsequent room until the hallway was a cacophony of shrill terror.

AFTERWORD

This story came to me as I was lying in bed one night, suffering from my first-ever bout of tinnitus. The buzzing sound made me think of a spider weaving a web in my brain with its lithe, sinewy legs. Its busy little body working tirelessly and in quick, tactile movements.

Welcome to my author brain, where the horrors I conjure up are woven into stories if they make the cut (or the seam, in this case).

I've always had a fascination with spiders and wanted to explore the nauseating realm of body horror as well. It really was quite exquisite how this story came to life, offering me the opportunity to weave these both together.

In fact, the beginning of the first chapter wherein Jenna sees the spindly silhouette of a spider was taken from an early memory of my own. I remember waking one night as a tiny tot and staring at a daddy longlegs on my comforter, just inches from my face. Its wiry figure was stark black against the glow of my nightlight. I was trembling in terror, and flung off my bedding, sending the spider flying to who knows where. I'm sure I slept with the lights on for the rest of the night. Since this was such a vivid memory from my childhood, it worked quite well to introduce Jenna's character and her arachnophobia.

There's just something about spiders, isn't there? Such a foreign, alien body with eight lithe appendages. They're truly remarkable creatures by design. Yet their ability to hide from sight and scuttle with seemingly unnatural ease makes them fearsome. And let's not even get into how large they can be; I'm sure you've heard of the Goliath birdeater and the giant huntsman spider.

For all of these reasons, however, they do tend to make good villains. We can say the same for sharks, alligators, and a plethora of other fascinating creatures. In reality, though, we know they are all living by survival instincts and evolutionary needs.

As this story fleshed itself out, I realized I couldn't use just any normal spider since they're not capable of crossing the bone and membrane barrier into the brain (thank goodness!). So therein lay my dilemma—how will this spider have come to be?

Ah, yes... To take a spider that can nimbly and efficiently crawl into your ear and design it as a weapon of mass destruction? The thought was absolutely horrifying—and perfect! My task at hand became clear, and I wove this narrative in.

I did my fair share of research finding just the right spider to use. Of course, I considered the black widow; this spider is iconic in the world of arachnids. Hell, it looks like a damn military weapon to me! But its too rigid and has too bulbous of an abdomen. Plus, its a bit overly big to pull this off. Once I came upon the *sac* spider, however, I knew I was onto something.

Let's just begin with the name, shall we? Sac spider... I don't know about you, but these two words put together are revolting. Plus, this spider species is quite innocuous. In fact, I'd never even heard of it until my research led to its discovery. What made this particular spider even more perfect was the fact that it's also a typical house spider and can be found just hanging out in the corners and crevices of homes.

Along the way, I included spiders here and there for fun... The arachnid Jenna encounters in the first chapter, and the giant house spiders she mentions during her doctor visit. It just so happened that these creatures existed exactly where I wanted them to for the twist in the end. And, of course, I had to look these spiders up. They're quite scary looking, but thankfully docile.

Jenna's appointment with her doctor was also based on a real-life experience. I had flown to Las Vegas with my family a few years back and suffered from tinnitus a couple weeks after returning. My ENT was very animated and cheerful, so in turn I wanted to write Jenna's ENT in the same fashion. The tinnitus has thankfully improved quite a bit, but I enjoyed weaving my experience into this story.

And that ending? Well, I love open endings that really hit hard and fill the reader with dread. Of course, we know what's going to happen next, and our imaginations have the opportunity to run wild with endless possibilities. How much of a chance do humans really have against combatting nimble and near-invisible spiderlings? Not much... And once each spiderling grows and harvests offspring of its own, it could be game over.

Creature features have always been popular and what I love about using real creatures is the impact it has on the story, essentially heightening the fear factor.

I've always had arachnophobia, and though it has become less debilitating as I get older, it's still there. Writing this story helped me overcome it a bit more.

While some spiders appear quite terrifying, their natural design is truly remarkable and they're just busy going about their spider business.

I hope you enjoyed *Spider*. Thank you so much for your support, and for taking the time to journey into my dark and twisted imagination for a little while.

Please consider leaving a review or rating—these really help support indie authors and allow our stories to get noticed, and I am extremely grateful for them.

Take care, Dear Reader... and be kind to our eight-legged friends.

ACKNOWLEDGEMENTS

It truly takes a village to bring a book to life, and I have so many people to thank.

Immense thanks to my husband and son, who carefully listen to my story concepts and offer critiques and advice. They are my world and I feel blessed beyond words to have their unwavering love and support.

Thank you to my dear friend, Steph, who loves horror just as much as I do. I know I can count on her for honest feedback and spirited conversation.

To my brother, Pete: Thank you for your valuable opinions and feedback. We've always both been very creative and fans of the horror genre.

Spider is dedicated to my brother, Bryan, who we lost in 2025. He left us way too soon. Though Bryan wasn't a horror fan, he loved hearing about my books and this story always made him cringe. Oh, but how he enjoyed hearing the updates! Bryan's beautiful spirit lives on.

Now moving on to the professional side of things:

Thanks to my wonderful editor, Sara Kelly. I can count on Sara to work her magic and leave me so many fun comments as well.

The cover of a book is so essential to capturing attention and conveying the story and I have my incredibly talented cover artist, Jelena Gajic, to thank for creating the cover art for *Spider*.

Further thanks to my beta readers and ARC readers. My beta readers offer such crucial feedback, and my ARC readers are invaluable for providing those early reviews that help so much to build exposure and interest.

To my social media families: Thank you for your tremendous support, kindness, and encouragement.

With gratitude,

Janelle

ALSO BY

Also by Janelle Schiecke
The Clatter Man
Death Cult
Ghost Room

ABOUT THE AUTHOR

Janelle Schiecke lives in New Jersey with her husband, her son, and their two cats. She has always reveled in everything spooky, and was raised on horror movies.

When she is not working on that next story, Janelle enjoys spending time with her family and friends, watching movies, reading with her cats snuggled up close, and family travel adventures.

You can follow Janelle on her social media accounts below:

Twitter/X: @J_Schiecke

Instagram: @janelle.schiecke

TikTok: @janelle.schiecke

For more information, including upcoming books, feel free to visit: www.janelleschiecke.com.

Join my author newsletter for updates, exclusives, and more: substack.com/@janelleschiecke.